The First Snowfall

Anne & Harlow Rockwell

ALADDIN BOOKS
MACMILLAN PUBLISHING COMPANY   NEW YORK
MAXWELL MACMILLAN CANADA   TORONTO
MAXWELL MACMILLAN INTERNATIONAL   NEW YORK OXFORD SINGAPORE SYDNEY

Aladdin Books   Maxwell Macmillan Canada, Inc.
Macmillan Publishing Company   1200 Eglinton Avenue East
866 Third Avenue   Suite 200
New York, NY 10022   Don Mills, Ontario M3C 3N1

Macmillan Publishing Company is part of the Maxwell
Communication Group of Companies.
Printed and bound in Hong Kong by South China Printing Company
(1988) Ltd.
10   9   8   7   6   5   4   3   2   1
The text of this book is set in 24 point Futura Book.
The illustrations are rendered in pencil and watercolor.
A hardcover edition of The First Snowfall is available from Macmillan
Publishing Company.

Library of Congress Cataloging-in-Publication Data
Rockwell, Anne F. The first snowfall / Anne & Harlow Rockwell. — 1st
Aladdin Books ed.   p.   cm.   Summary: A child enjoys the special
sights and activities of a snow-covered world. ISBN 0-689-71614-1
1. Snow—Juvenile literature.   [1. Snow.]   I.Rockwell, Harlow.
II. Title.   [QC926.37.R63   1992]   551.57.'84—dc20   91-41247

I saw the snow begin to fall.

Snow fell and fell
all through the cold and quiet night.

In the morning, I put on
red mittens, a plaid muffler,
my woolly cap, and warm boots

with my
new ski jacket
and pants.

Then I went outside
in the snow.

I waved to the driver
of the snowplow
when it came down our street.

This is the snow shovel
I used

to shovel a path through the snow.

This is the snowball I rolled

to build our snowman.

Our car was covered with snow
until we brushed it off.

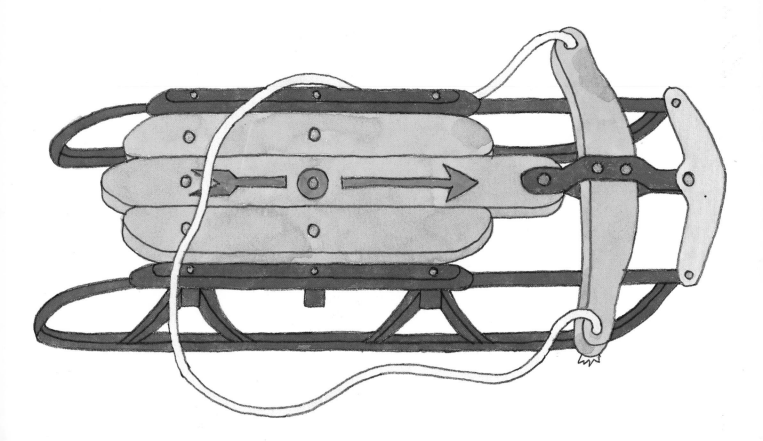

This is the sled
we put in the car.

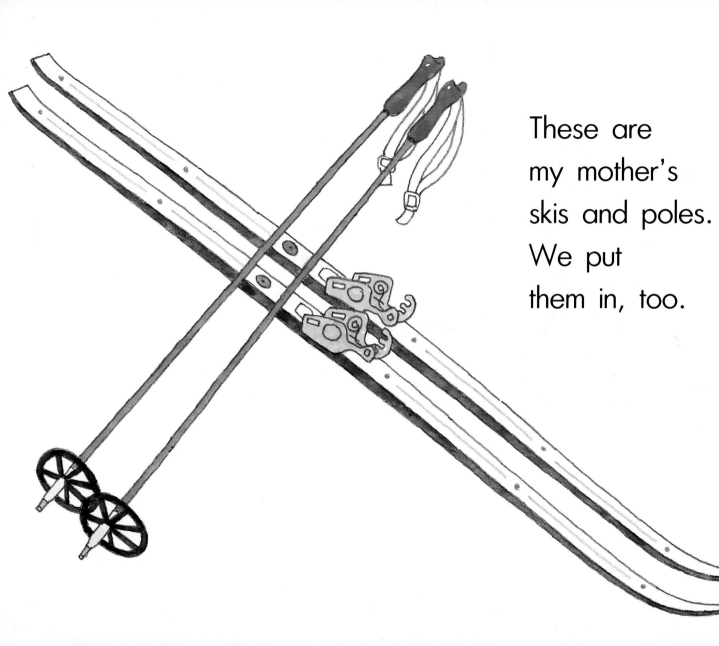

These are
my mother's
skis and poles.
We put
them in, too.

At the park,
I rode
on the sled
with my father.

My mother
skied across the hills
all covered with snow.

This is the hot cocoa
I drank
when I came home.

It warmed me up.

Then I went outside
to play in the snow some more.